A Gift For:

_____

From:

_____

Published by Hallmark Gift Books,
a division of Hallmark Cards, Inc.,
Kansas City, MO 64141
Visit us on the Web at www.Hallmark.com.

Editor: Emily Osborn
Art Director: Kevin Swanson
Designer: Brian Pilachowski
Production Designer: Bryan Ring

ISBN: 978-1-59530-444-5
BOK1186

Printed and bound in China
SEP11

Tickle Me!

BY Melissa Woo

GIFT BOOKS

Everyone in Tickle Town
is tickled that you're here!
They love to get their giggle on
all throughout the year!

Grouchy-pants are not allowed!

No pouting, frowns or prickles!

All you'll find in their fun town are

laughter,

smiles

and
tickles!

Whenever Piggie plays in mud,

her giggler gets so giggly!

She
chuckles,

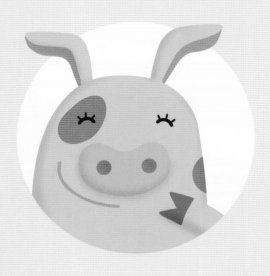

snickers,

even snorts!

She gets all wiggly-jiggly!

Do YOU have a ticklish belly?

When I laugh,
mine jiggles like jelly!

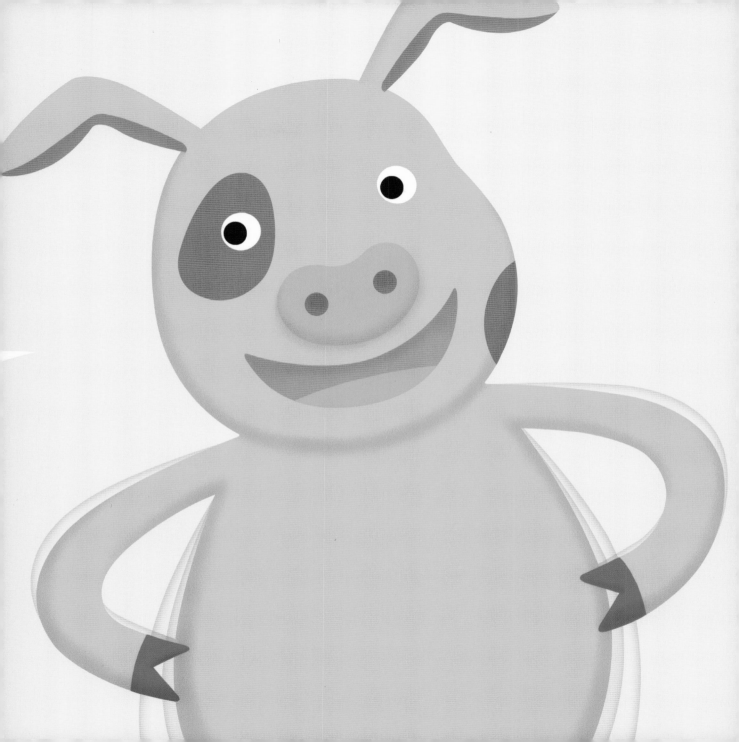

Monkey's toes
feel tickly
as he swings
from tree to tree.

He goes bananas chuckling,

"Ooh-
ha-ha!
Hee-
hee-
hee!"

Do YOU have ticklish toes?

Donkey's hee-haw happy—

he's the most ticklish of them all!

Behind his ears! Below his chin!

He laughs until he falls!

Do YOU have ticklish ears?

Where else are you ticklish?

Everyone in Tickle Town
is tickled you stopped by!
So go and get YOUR giggle on—
it's easy if you try!

If you were tickled pink by this book,

we would love to hear from you!

Please send your comments to:

Hallmark Book Feedback

P.O. Box 419034

Mail Drop 215

Kansas City, MO 64141

Or e-mail us at:

booknotes@hallmark.com